Editors: Ann Redpath, Etienne Delessert
Art Director: Rita Marshall
Publisher: George R. Peterson, Jr.

Copyright © 1984 Creative Education, Inc., 123 S. Broad Street,
Mankato, Minnesota 56001, USA. American Edition.
Copyright © 1984 Grasset & Fasquelle, Paris – Editions 24 Heures, Lausanne. French Edition.
International copyrights reserved in all countries.

Library of Congress Catalog Card No.: 83-71175
Rumanian Fairy Tale, The Enchanted Pig
Mankato, MN: Creative Education, Inc.; 40 pages. ISBN: 0-87191-953-2

Color separations by Photolitho A.G., Gossau/Zurich
Printed in Switzerland by Imprimeries Réunies S.A. Lausanne.

THE
ENCHANTED
PIG

RUMANIAN FAIRY TALE
illustrated by
JACQUES TARDI

CREATIVE EDUCATION INC.

ONCE UPON A TIME

THERE was a King who had three daughters. Now it happened that he had to go out to battle, so he called his daughters and said to them:

"My dear children, I am obliged to go to the wars. The enemy is approaching us with a large army. It is a great grief to me to leave you all. During my absence take care of yourselves and be good girls. Look after everything in the house. You may walk in the garden, and you may go into all the rooms in the palace, except the room at the back in the right-hand corner. You must not enter it, for harm would befall you."

"You may keep your mind easy, father," they replied. "We have never been disobedient to you. Go in peace, and may heaven give you a glorious victory!"

When everything was ready for his departure, the King gave them the keys of all the rooms and reminded them once more of what he had said. His daughters kissed his hands with tears in their eyes, and wished him prosperity.

Now when the girls found themselves alone they felt so sad that they did not know what to do. To pass the time, they decided to work for part of the day, to read for part of the day, and to enjoy themselves in the garden for part of the day. But every day they grew more and more curious.

"Sisters," said the eldest Princess, "all day long we sew, spin, and read. We have been several days quite alone. We have been in all the rooms of our father's palace, and have admired the beautiful furniture: why should we not go into the room that our father forbad us to enter?"

"Sister," said the youngest, "I cannot think how you can tempt us to break our father's command. When he told us not to go into that room he must have known what he was saying."

"Surely the sky won't fall about our heads if we *do* go in," said the second Princess. "How will our father ever find out that we have gone in?"

While they were speaking thus, encouraging each other, they had reached the room. The eldest fitted the key into the lock, and snap! the door stood open.

The three girls entered, and what do you think they saw?

The room was quite empty, but in the middle stood a large table, and on it lay a big open book.

Now the Princesses were curious to know what was written in the book, especially the eldest, and this is what she read:

"The eldest daughter of this King will marry a prince from the East."

Then the second girl stepped forward, and turning over the page she read:

"The second daughter of this King will marry a prince from the West."

But the youngest Princess did not want to go near the table or to open the book. Her elder sisters dragged her up to the table, and in fear and trembling she turned the page and read:

"The youngest daughter of this King will be married to a pig from the North."

Now if a thunderbolt had fallen upon her, it would not have frightened her more. She almost died of misery. Her sisters tried to comfort her, saying:

"How can you believe such nonsense? When did it ever happen that a king's daughter married a pig?"

The youngest Princess would fain have let herself be convinced by her sisters' words. But her thoughts kept turning to the book.

Besides, the thought weighed on her heart that she had been guilty of disobeying her father. She began to get quite ill, and in a few days she was so changed that it was difficult to recognize her. Formerly she had been rosy and merry, now she was pale and nothing gave her any joy. She gave up playing with her sisters in the garden, and ceased to gather flowers to put in her hair.

However, it was not long before the King noticed that his third daughter was getting very thin and sad-looking. And all of a sudden it flashed through his mind that she had disobeyed his word. To be quite certain he called his daughters to him, and ordered them to speak the truth. They confessed everything.

The King was so distressed when he heard it that he was almost overcome by grief.

In the meantime the King won a great victory, and he hurried home to his daughters, to whom his thoughts had constantly turned. Everyone went out to meet him, and there was great rejoicing. The King's first act on reaching home was to thank Heaven for his victory. He then entered his palace, and his joy was great when he saw that the Princesses were all well, for the youngest did her best not to appear sad.

Well, these events had almost been forgotten when one fine day a prince from the East appeared at the Court and asked the King for the hand of his eldest daughter. The King gladly gave his consent. A great wedding banquet was prepared, and soon after the happy pair were accompanied to the frontier.

After some time the same thing befell the second daughter, who was wooed and won by a prince from the West.

When the young Princess saw that everything fell out exactly as had been written in the book, she grew very sad. She refused to eat, and would not put on her fine clothes. She declared that she would rather die than become a laughingstock to the world. But the King would not allow her to do anything so wrong, and he comforted her in every way.

Now the King was astonished to hear so fine a speech from a Pig, and at once it occurred to him that something strange was the matter. When he heard that the Court and the whole street were full of all the pigs in the world, the King saw that he must give his consent to the wedding. The Pig would not go away till the King had sworn a royal oath upon it.

The King then sent for his daughter, and advised her to submit to fate, as there was nothing else to be done. And he added:

"My child, the words and whole behavior of this Pig are quite unlike those of other pigs. I do not myself believe that he always *was* a pig. I think that some magic or witchcraft has been at work. Obey him, and do everything that he wishes, and I feel sure that Heaven will shortly send you release."

So the time passed, till lo and behold! one fine day an enormous pig from the North walked into the palace, and going straight up to the King said, "Hail O King!" May your life be as prosperous and bright as sunrise on a clear day!"

"I am glad to see you well, friend," answered the King, "but what wind has brought you hither?"

"I come a-wooing," replied the Pig.

"If you wish me to do this, dear father, I will do it," replied the girl.

After the marriage, the Pig and his bride set out for his home in a royal carriage. On the way they passed a great bog, and the Pig got out and rolled about in the mire till he was covered with mud. Then he got back into the carriage and told his wife to kiss him. She bethought herself of her father's words and, pulling out her pocket handkerchief, she gently wiped the Pig's snout and kissed it.

By the time they reached the Pig's dwelling, it was quite dark. They had supper together, and lay down to rest. During the night the Princess noticed that the Pig had changed into a man. She was not a little surprised, but she decided to wait and see what would happen.

And now she noticed that every night the Pig became a man, and every morning he was changed into a Pig before she awoke. Clearly her husband must be bewitched. In time she grew quite fond of him, he was so kind and gentle.

One day as she was sitting alone she saw an old witch go past. She felt quite excited, as it was so long since she had seen a human being. The witch told her that she understood all magic arts, and that she knew the healing powers of herbs and plants.

"Can you tell me," asked the Princess, "why my husband is a Pig by day and a human being by night?"

"If you like, I will give you an herb to break the spell, my dear, said the witch. "At night, when your husband is asleep, get up very quietly, and fasten this thread round his left foot as firmly as possible. You will see in the morning he will not have changed back into a Pig. I do not want any reward. I shall be repaid by knowing that you are happy.

When the old witch had gone away the Princess hid the thread very carefully, and at night she got up quietly, and with a beating heart she bound the thread round her husband's foot. Just as she was pulling the knot tight there was a crack, and the thread broke, for it was rotten.

Her husband awoke and said, "Unhappy woman, what have you done? Three days more and this unholy spell would have been over. Now, who knows how long I may have to be in this disgusting shape? I must leave you at once. We shall not meet again until you have worn out three pairs of iron shoes and blunted a steel staff in your search for me." Then he disappeared.

Now the Princess began to weep. But when she saw that her tears did her no good, she got up, determined to go wherever fate should lead her.

On reaching a town, the first thing she did was to order three pairs of iron sandals and a steel staff. Then she set out in search of her husband. She wandered over nine seas and across nine continents; through thick forests; the boughs of the trees hit her face, and the shrubs tore her hands, but on she went, and never looked back. At last, wearied but still with hope at her heart, she reached a house.

Now who do you think lived there? The Moon.

The Princess knocked and begged to be let in. The mother of the Moon, felt a great pity for her, and took her in and nursed and tended her. And while she was here the Princess had a little baby.

One day the mother of the Moon asked her:

"How was it possible for you, a mortal, to get hither to the house of the Moon?"

Then the Princess told her all that happened, and added: "I shall always be thankful to you that you took pity on me and on my baby. Now I beg one last favor of you; can your daughter, the Moon, tell me where my husband is?"

"She cannot tell you that," replied the goddess, "but, if you will travel towards the East until you reach the dwelling of the Sun, he may be able to tell you something."

Then she gave the Princess a roast chicken to eat, and warned her to be very careful not to lose any of the bones, because they might be of great use to her.

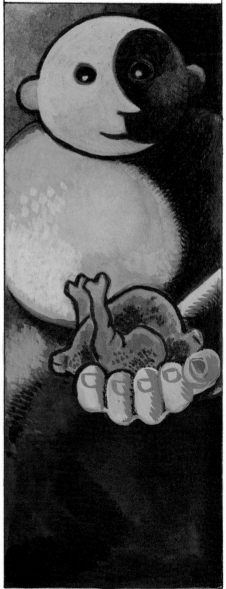

When the Princess had
thanked her and had thrown
away one pair of shoes that
were worn out, she tied up the
chicken bones in a bundle, and
taking her baby in her arms
and her staff in her hand, she
set out once more.

She went across bare sandy deserts; she crossed high rocky mountains, jumping from crag to crag. She had to cross swamps and to scale mountain peaks covered with flints, so that her feet and knees and elbows were all torn and bleeding. Sometimes she came to a precipice across which she could not jump, and she had to crawl round on hands and knees, helping herself along with her staff.

At length, she reached the palace in which the Sun lived. The mother of the Sun was astonished at beholding a mortal from earth, and wept when she heard of all she had suffered. Then, having promised to ask her son about the Princess's husband, she hid her in the cellar, so that the Sun might notice nothing on his return home, for he was always in a bad temper when he came in at night.

The next day the Princess feared that things would not go well with her, for the Sun had noticed that someone from the other world had been in the palace.

"How in the world is it possible for the Sun to be angry? He is so beautiful and so good to mortals," she asked.

"This is how it happens," replied the Sun's mother. "In the morning when he stands at the gates of paradise he is happy, and smiles on the whole world, but during the day he gets cross, because he sees all the evil deeds of men, and that is why his heat becomes so scorching; but in the evening he is sad and angry, for he stands at the gates of death. Then he comes back here."

She then told the Princess that she had asked about her husband, but her son had replied that he knew nothing about him, and that her only hope was to go and inquire of the Wind.

Before the Princess left, the mother of the Sun gave her a roast chicken to eat, and advised her to take great care of the bones. She then threw away her second pair of shoes, which were quite worn out, and with her child on her arm and her staff in her hand, she set forth on her way to the Wind.

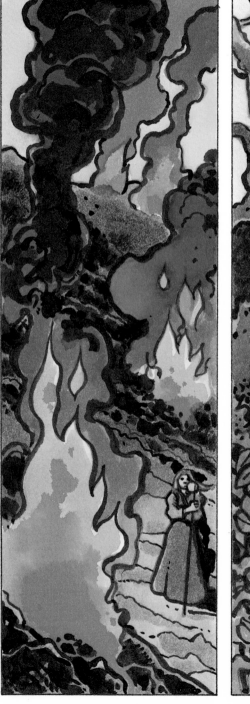

In these wanderings she met with even greater difficulties than before, for she came upon one mountain of flints after another, out of which tongues of fire would flame up; she had to cross fields of ice and avalanches of snow. The poor woman nearly died of these hardships, but she kept a brave heart, and at length she reached an enormous cave in the side of a mountain. This was where the Wind lived. There was a little door in front of the cave, and the Princess knocked, begging for admission. The mother of the Wind had pity on her and took her in. Here too she was hidden away, so that the Wind might not notice her.

The next morning the mother of the Wind told her that her husband was living in a thick wood. Here he had built himself a house of tree trunks and here he lived alone, shunning humankind.

After the mother of the Wind had given the Princess a chicken to eat, and had warned her to take care of the bones, she advised her to go by the Milky Way, which at night lies across the sky, and to wander on till she reached her goal.

Having thanked the old woman, the Princess set out on her journey and rested neither night nor day, so great was her longing to see her husband.

On and on she walked until her last pair of shoes fell in pieces. So she threw them away and went on with bare feet, not heeding the bogs nor the thorns that wounded her. At last she reached a beautiful, green meadow on the edge of a wood. Her heart was cheered by the sight of the flowers. She sat down and rested for a little. But hearing the birds chirping to their mates among the trees made her think with longing of her husband, and she wept bitterly, and taking her child in her arms, and her bundle of chicken bones on her shoulder, she entered the wood.

For three days and three nights she struggled through it. She was quite worn out with weariness and hunger, and even her staff was no further help to her, for in her wanderings it had become quite blunted. She almost gave up but made one last great effort. Suddenly in a thicket she came upon the house that the mother of the Wind had described. It had no windows, and the door was up in the roof. Round the house she went, in search of steps, but could find none. She tried in vain to climb up to the door. Then suddenly she thought of the chicken bones that she had dragged all that weary way, and she said to herself: "They would not all have told me to take such good care of these bones if they had not had some good reason for doing so."

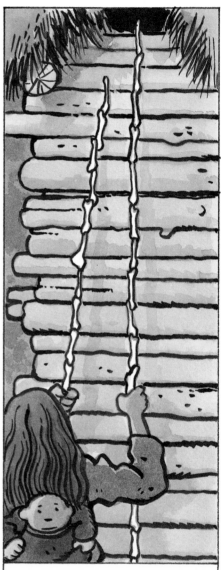

So she took the bones out of
her bundle, and she placed the
two ends together. To her sur-
prise they stuck tight; then she
added the other bones, till she
had two long poles the height
of the house; these she placed
against the wall, at a distance

of a yard from one another.
Across them she placed the
other bones, piece by piece,
like the steps of a ladder. As
soon as one step was finished
she stood upon it and made
the next one, till she was close
to the door. But just as she got

near the top she noticed that there were no bones left for the last rung of the ladder. Then suddenly an idea came to her. Taking a knife, she chopped off her little finger, and placing it on the last step, it stuck as the bones had done.

The ladder was complete, and with her child on her arm she entered the door of the house. Here she found everything in perfect order. She laid the child down to sleep in a trough that was on the floor, and sat down herself to rest.

When her husband, the Pig, came back to his house, he could not believe his eyes. He stared at the ladder of bones, and at the little finger on the top of it. He felt that some fresh magic must be at work, and in his terror, he changed himself into a dove, so that no witchcraft could have power over him. He flew into the room and here he found a woman rocking a child. At the sight of her, looking so changed by all that she had suffered for his sake, his heart was moved by such love and longing and by so great a pity that he suddenly became a man.

The Princess stood up when she saw him, and her heart beat with fear, for she did not know him. But when he had told her who he was, in her great joy she forgot all her sufferings, and they seemed as nothing to her. He was a very handsome man. They sat down together and she told him all her adventures, and he wept with pity at the tale. And then he told her his own history.

"I am a King's son. Once when my father was fighting against some dragons, I slew the youngest dragon. His mother, who was a witch, cast a spell and changed me into a Pig.

It was she who gave you the thread to bind round my foot. So that instead of the three days I was forced to remain a Pig for three more years. Now that we have suffered for each other, and have found each other again, let us forget the past."

And in their joy they kissed one another.

Next morning they set out early to return to his father's kingdom. His father and his mother embraced them both, and there was feasting in the palace for three days and three nights.

Then they set out to see her father. When she had told him all her adventures, he said to her:

"Did not I tell you that I was quite sure that the creature who won you as his wife had not been born a Pig? You were wise in doing as I told you."

And as the King was old and had no heirs, he put them on the throne in his place. And they ruled as only kings rule who have suffered many things. And if they are not dead they are still living and ruling happily.

Concord
South Side